ARAX THE SOUL STEALER

year 3

With special thanks to Jan Burchett and Sara Vogler

For Will Kirk, with lots of love from Jan and Sara

www.beastquest.co.uk

ORCHARD BOOKS
338 Euston Road, London NW1 3BH
Orchard Books Australia
Level 17/207 Kent St, Sydney, NSW 2000

A Paperback Original
First published in Great Britain in 2009

Beast Quest is a registered trademark of Working Partners Limited
Series created by Working Partners Limited, London

Text © Working Partners Limited 2009
Cover and inside illustrations by Steve Sims © Orchard Books 2009

A CIP catalogue record for this book is available from the British Library.

ISBN 978 1 40830 382 5

3 5 7 9 10 8 6 4

Printed in Great Britain by CPI Bookmarque, Croydon

The paper and board used in this paperback are natural recyclable products made from wood grown in sustainable forests. The manufacturing processes conform to the environmental regulations of the country of origin.

Orchard Books is a division of Hachette Children's Books, an Hachette UK company.

www.hachette.co.uk

ARAX THE SOUL STEALER

BY ADAM BLADE

THE ICY P
THE NORTHERN MOUNTAINS
THE
WESTERN OCEAN
THE FOREST OF FEAR
THE

Avantia
GRASSY PLAINS
KING HUGO'S PALACE
THE CITY
ERRINEL

A FRIEND LOST

Dear Friend,

Allow me to introduce myself. I am Marc, apprentice to Aduro, the great wizard of Avantia. I do not have much time to talk to you – my master is in great danger and I must urgently return to his side. Malvel has brought his greatest power yet to bear on him, and the consequences for the kingdom may be terrible. I hope that my magic and Aduro's expertise will be enough to keep the evil wizard's spells at bay. But we may still need a hero's help…

I have heard much about the boy, Tom, and his Quests. I fear he is about to face his greatest challenge yet – to save his friend, and protect Avantia. Time is running out and Aduro will soon be lost forever, unless Tom can defeat the most dreadful Beast of all…

Farewell for now,

Marc, apprentice to Aduro

CHAPTER ONE

THE SILENT PALACE

Tom woke suddenly. It was quiet and for a moment he couldn't think where he was. He sat up, rubbing his eyes, and looked around. He was on a soft, warm mattress in a large room. Sunlight streamed in through narrow arched windows.

Of course! Now I remember, he thought. He and Elenna were back at

King Hugo's palace after another successful Beast Quest.

It made a change to wake up in a comfortable bed. During their Quests he had got used to sleeping in caves or under the stars.

Tom glowed at the thought that King Hugo had chosen him to fight the evil Wizard Malvel and his fearsome Beasts, which threatened to destroy the kingdom of Avantia. The night before, at the great feast held in honour of him and Elenna, the King had told the whole court how proud he was of them both. Tom had thought he would burst with happiness.

He jumped up and shook Elenna, who was still asleep in her bed under the window.

"Come on, sleepyhead," he urged,

tugging at her blanket. "King Hugo must have let us sleep in. Let's go and see if there's anything left for breakfast."

Elenna appeared from under her tangle of bedclothes, her close-cropped hair looking spikier than ever. Then she grinned and leapt to her feet. "Race you there!"

A few moments later, they were charging down the staircase to the Great Hall. But Tom suddenly stopped in his tracks. Elenna nearly tumbled into him.

"Whoa!" she gasped, recovering herself. "What's the matter?"

Tom swung round to face her. "What can you hear, Elenna?"

His friend shrugged. "Nothing. It's really quiet."

"Exactly!" declared Tom. "The sun's

up – the palace should be busy by now."

"You're right," said Elenna thoughtfully. "We haven't even seen a servant." She stared out of a window. "The courtyard is completely deserted. There's usually someone practising at the archery butts."

"There must be people somewhere," said Tom, puzzled. "Let's look."

The Great Hall lay silent and still. The King's throne was empty and the breakfast tables were bare. There wasn't even a fire in the grate.

"It feels as if we're the only people alive," whispered Tom. Their footsteps echoed as they moved cautiously across the flagstones.

"It's really spooky," agreed Elenna.

They reached the steps leading down to the kitchens. Normally the sound of chatter and the smell of freshly baked bread would greet them. But today there was nothing.

"No one's even lit the torches downstairs," said Elenna.

Suddenly a nearby door was flung open. It clanged against the stone wall, making them jump.

"Who goes there?" demanded a booming voice. A grim-faced guard strode into the Great Hall, his sword drawn.

"Tom and Elenna," said Tom quickly. "Guests of the King."

The man sheathed his sword. "I was on my way to find you," he said. "I have orders from King Hugo. You are to go to Aduro's chambers immediately."

"What's going on?" asked Elenna. "Where is everyone?"

"They are all in their own rooms," answered the guard. "By order of the King. The palace is not safe. That's all I can tell you."

Tom and Elenna ran to the spiral staircase that led up the palace's tallest turret. Wizard Aduro had his private quarters at the very top.

"We've never been allowed near Aduro's rooms before," panted Tom, as he raced up the steps. "Normally we're forbidden even to set foot in the tower."

At last they reached the top. Ahead of them was a studded wooden door. A picture of Aduro's staff was painted on it, surrounded by a circle of moons. Tom could see a strange glow around the door's edges. Elenna glanced at him questioningly.

Tom raised his hand to knock. But an unearthly roar from inside the room made him start back.

"Aduro!" he gasped. "He's in danger."

"Then we must help him," said Elenna.

They stood for a moment with their weapons raised, then Tom kicked open the door and they ran inside.

A figure was crouched in the far corner of the chamber. Tom could see its wild eyes and bared teeth. Hissing and growling, it was being watched closely by two of King Hugo's guards. The figure had the same strange glow about it that had seeped from under the door. It was the only light in the dark room.

"Where's Aduro?" Tom shouted to the guards.

Elenna gave a sudden cry and pointed to the writhing figure. The guards now had a firm grasp on the creature's arms. "It's wearing Aduro's robes!" she exclaimed. "But that's not possible! It can't be..."

Tom stared in horror. The evil, twisted figure before them was Aduro, the good wizard of Avantia. But there was none of the usual wisdom and kindness in his gaze. His face was twisted with venom. His eyes blazed furiously beneath his wild, matted hair. The veins on his arms stood out like gnarled roots as he thrashed about, trying to free himself.

Suddenly, Aduro thrust aside the guards and leapt at Tom with a chilling snarl.

CHAPTER TWO

ADURO THE BAD

Aduro's grasping fingers snatched at Tom's face, forcing him to leap out of reach. The guards grabbed hold of the wizard and pulled him away. He writhed and struggled in their strong grip. Then he gave an unearthly howl of anger.

"Keep back, Tom," warned Elenna, her voice trembling.

"Something terrible has happened!" said Tom. "I have to find out what it is. The King may also be in danger."

"I am safe," said a voice behind him. Tom whirled round to see King Hugo emerge from the shadows. Aduro's new apprentice, Marc, was by his side. Tom was shocked at how pale and worried they both looked. The King leant heavily on a table that was covered in Aduro's books and potions. His hands trembled as he spoke.

"Once again, the kingdom needs your help, Tom and Elenna," he said gravely. "As you can see, there has been a terrible change in our good wizard."

Aduro's thin, gloating laugh filled the room. "Your King is going to send you on a Quest!" he hissed, wrenching an arm free and jabbing a finger at Tom. "A Quest that will prove too much for you, Tom. You will fail."

Tom felt a shiver run through him. Aduro's voice was full of loathing. He couldn't believe that his friend was saying such terrible things. The wizard had always trusted Tom before and believed he would fulfil every Quest.

"Malvel must have done this to Aduro!" Tom said.

"I fear you are right," said King Hugo, his voice tight with emotion. "Do you remember how Malvel stole the golden armour?"

Tom nodded. "He sent a flock of evil bats to steal it from the palace armoury. They carried it away in their claws."

"I have never seen one of Malvel's Beasts," said King Hugo, "but those bats were enough to give me a taste of how dangerous the evil sorcerer can be. And now I fear he has conjured up a Beast that is truly terrifying." He gestured to Aduro's apprentice.

Marc stepped forwards, looking nervous. The young man had only just begun to study under Aduro.

"*Venellor akona weyull,*" he muttered under his breath. Then he gestured with his hands. A terrifying image formed in the air before them.

"It looks like a giant bat," gasped Elenna.

In the vision shimmered a Beast. It had the head of a man, with twisted horns jutting from its temples and cruel eyes staring from its bony, skull-like face. Its leathery bat wings stretched out, as if it were about to engulf some invisible prey. One of the clawed fists at the end of its muscular arms held a vicious-looking whip. The Beast hovered in the air, hissing fiercely.

"It's horrible," said Tom.

"There's more," Marc told him. The apprentice clicked his fingers and the vision changed. Now Tom and Elenna could see an image of Aduro. He looked wise and kind – nothing like the hunched, raging monster in the corner of the room. In the floating picture the Beast swooped down from the sky. Tom cried out in horror.

The Beast cracked its whip. Before Aduro could act, the long leather coil flew out towards him, barbs jutting from its sides. The barbs ripped through his robe and bit deep into the flesh just above his heart. Aduro gave a cry of anguish and fell to the ground.

Tom felt Elenna clutch his arm as coils of purple smoke emerged from the puncture wounds in Aduro's body. They swirled in the air, then floated towards the Beast and were absorbed into his body. Tom could see that as the smoke left Aduro, the light of goodness faded from the wizard's eyes. A look of pure venom smouldered there in its place.

Marc waved his hands and the vision disappeared. No one spoke for a moment.

"You have seen the most terrible thing that could happen in Avantia," said King Hugo. "The Beast has stolen Aduro's soul – his wisdom and honesty, his decency and kindness."

"But that is the very heart of Aduro's magic," exclaimed Tom. "Without it, he can't protect Avantia!"

"I think that's exactly what Malvel intended," explained King Hugo. "This Beast has the power to steal all the good qualities from any person it attacks, leaving only the bad behind." He picked up a box. "I must show you something else." He opened the lid and pulled out a scrap of linen. "The Beast left this."

Tom took the cloth from him and looked it over. "My name is sewn onto this," he said, feeling a tingle of dread.

"It's like the square of linen you found in the castle where you defeated Kaymon the gorgon hound," said Elenna. "The one that your father left for you. That had your name on it, too."

"This is from someone very different," said the King. "Look closer."

Tom peered at the piece of cloth.

"It's horrible!" he cried. "See here, Elenna. It's stained with drops of blood. And my name's not embroidered with thread – it's embroidered with human hair!"

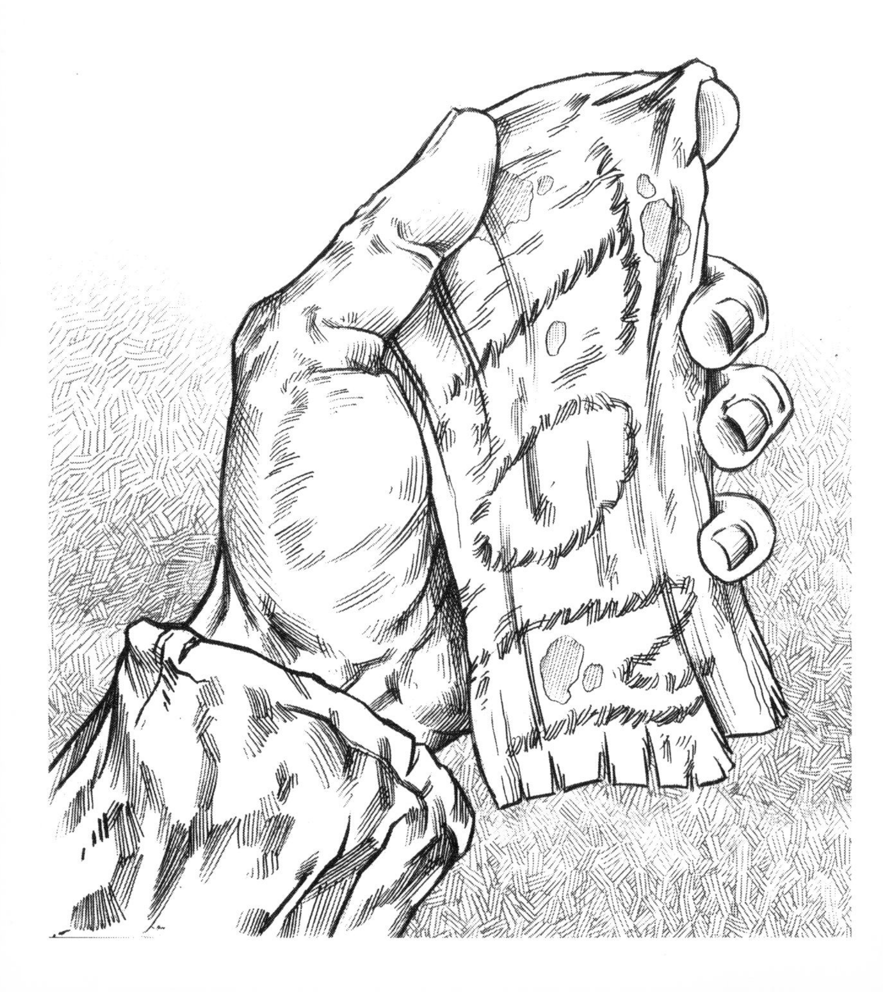

There was a shriek of ugly laughter from Aduro, who was still hunched in the corner of the room.

"Beware, Tom," he snarled, "for that can mean only one thing." He flashed a smile of pure evil. "The Beast will be after you next!"

Tom felt a shiver of icy fear go up his spine.

CHAPTER THREE

A NEW QUEST!

Aduro snarled and thrashed against his captors, lashing wildly at Tom. The guards were struggling hard to restrain him.

"He's so strong!" gasped Elenna in disbelief.

"It must come from the evil inside him," said Tom.

King Hugo quickly led Tom and

Elenna out of the room. He took Tom by the shoulders and stared gravely into his eyes. "I am going to send you on a Quest. It will call for the utmost bravery. You must find and defeat this new Beast of Malvel's – before it wreaks more damage on our kingdom."

"You can count on me," declared Tom. Elenna nodded in eager agreement.

"It warms my heart to hear you say that," said King Hugo. Then he sighed deeply. "Avantia needs its wizard back. If the Beast is not defeated, I fear that Aduro will be lost to us forever."

"We can't let that happen," said Elenna.

"No, we can't!" said Tom fiercely. "If we lose Aduro and his magic, the Kingdom of Avantia will be at Malvel's mercy. The Beast must have come into the palace last night to attack Aduro. Why didn't he come for me then?"

"You know better than most the ways of Malvel," King Hugo answered. "I fear he must be turning this into an evil game – and he intends that foul Beast to be the winner." He stroked his beard thoughtfully. "Yours will be a fearsome task," he went on. "Take the greatest of care and fight bravely. Avantia depends on you. You are the only person that stands in the way of Malvel's final victory over us all."

Tom felt a surge of power run through him. He knew what he had to do. "While there is blood in my veins, I will save Aduro and Avantia."

"We are ready, King Hugo," said Elenna. Tom gave her a grateful look. It was always comforting to know he had such a loyal friend.

The two of them made their way down the turret's steep spiral staircase. Tom glanced over his shoulder to give a farewell wave to the King, who stood with his shoulders stooped. Tom had never seen him look so defeated.

A sudden gust of icy wind blew at them. Elenna shivered.

A high-pitched whisper stabbed like knives into Tom's head. "Arax the Soul Stealer will find you!"

His hands flew to his ears. Tom knew that voice only too well. It was Malvel.

"Arax..." repeated Tom, fighting down a shudder of fear. "Arax will be defeated – just like all the other

Beasts you've sent to Avantia! Do you hear me, Malvel?"

With an angry cry, the icy wind swirled away down the staircase.

Tom leapt down the last few steps and out into the deserted palace courtyard. He was glad to feel the warmth of the sun on his face. Elenna bounded after him.

“Are you all right, Tom?” she asked anxiously.

Tom nodded his head. “Malvel was just trying to frighten me.” He grinned at her. “He’ll have to try a lot harder than that. Now I know the name of the Beast – Arax.”

They made for the stables to find Storm and Silver, their faithful companions.

Storm, Tom's black stallion, whinnied a greeting and pushed against his stable door.

"I think he knows we're off on another Quest!" laughed Tom.

There was a bark of welcome and the furry grey head and paws of Elenna's pet wolf, Silver, appeared over the stable door. Elenna scratched him between the ears.

"You're coming too, boy," she said affectionately.

Tom unlatched the door and saddled Storm ready for the journey. Silver dashed round the courtyard, barking with excitement.

"There's just one question," said Elenna. "Where do we find this new Beast? He could be anywhere."

"My map will tell us," said Tom. He began to unfurl it, and then hesitated. “Although we may have a problem. Aduro gave this map to me. Will it be any use without his good magic?”

“There’s only one way to find out,” Elenna told him.

Together they unrolled the map and laid it out on the courtyard cobbles. Tom knelt over it.

For a moment the parchment looked blank. Then, to Tom’s relief, a picture of Avantia appeared. He could see the Western Ocean, its waves lapping at the shore, his home village of Errinel, nestling in the southeast, and King Hugo’s palace, right in the centre of the city.

“Yes!” he exclaimed. “The map’s magic is still working.”

“Then Arax must be on the map,” Elenna said, kneeling beside Tom,

Avantia
RAINFOREST
DENSE FOREST
THE RIVER
MARSHES
CITY GATES
WELL

"but I can't see any sign of him."

The two friends scanned the miniature landscape.

"Look!" cried Tom suddenly. His finger flew to the mountains. They were covered in heavy dark clouds, which swirled away as he touched them. "Can you see that black shape over the peaks?"

Elenna nodded eagerly. "That's him!"

Silver gave an excited bark.

The two friends watched the tiny shape of Arax circle the jagged spurs. Then the image of the Beast swooped down and seemed to disappear into the rock.

Elenna jumped up. "We should have guessed that's where he'd be. Arax is a bat – and bats live in caves. There must be hundreds of caves up there for him to hide in."

"That's where he'll be waiting for us!" Tom declared, scrambling to his feet. "Let's go."

CHAPTER FOUR

TO THE MOUNTAIN

Tom leapt onto Storm's back and Elenna jumped up behind him. Silver bounded across the empty palace courtyard and Storm set off at an eager trot.

"You wouldn't think we'd only just returned from a Quest," laughed Tom. "They're both so full of energy!"

Soon they were through the city

and out of the gates. Tom turned back and looked at the purple spires and sea-green domes of King Hugo's palace. He had a heavy feeling in his heart. Would he ever see the palace again? Elenna put a hand on his shoulder.

"This is a tough Quest," she said. "But if anyone can overcome this Beast, it's you."

"Thanks, Elenna," he replied.

Tom flicked open his compass. It had been a gift from his father, Taladon the Swift. Taladon had disappeared when Tom was a baby, so Tom had no memories of him. But the compass was one of his most treasured possessions.

"The mountain's west of here," he said. He pointed over the flat, grassy plains.

They rode for the whole morning without a rest. Silver kept darting eagerly ahead, then ran back to wait for them. By late afternoon the plains had given way to rocky slopes and they could see the mountain in the distance, dark and brooding.

"It looks so threatening," said Elenna grimly. "A perfect home for one of Malvel's Beasts."

"Not for much longer!" answered Tom.

Storm had dropped to a slow trot. Tom patted his stallion's neck, then leant to one side to survey the ground.

"These foothills are hard-going for Storm," he said. "The loose rocks are slippery under his hooves. I wish we could stop for a rest, boy, but there's no time."

Silver was no longer bounding ahead, but plodded along, panting deeply, his tongue hanging out. The mountain peaks were a blackish purple against the twilight. Then Tom heard a faint rushing sound.

"There must be water nearby," he said.

He reined Storm in and twisted in the saddle to listen. "It's on the other side of those trees. We must have reached the Winding River. That'll be an ideal place to make camp."

"Good idea," said Elenna, slipping to the ground. "It'll be dark soon. I'll catch some fish for supper."

Tom dismounted and led Storm in the direction Elenna had taken. He could see the river now. The shallow water twisted and turned around the rocks of the foothills, glinting in the twilight. Elenna was already on the riverbank, staring into it intently.

"Tom!" he heard her call in alarm. "Come quickly!"

Tom dropped Storm's reins and ran to join her. The river was pounding down the rocks from the mountain, the waves churning up white foam. But something strange was happening. Hundreds of fish were leaping out from the spray in a seething mass. They seemed to be trying to reach the bank. Some already lay on the grass and were flapping, mouths open.

"What's the matter with them?" gasped Elenna. "Why would they want to escape? They'll die."

"I've no idea," said Tom, frowning. "But I don't like it." Gently he picked up one of the flapping fish and put it back in the water. To his surprise, the fish jerked and thrashed about, then jumped straight back onto the grass again.

"Perhaps there's something wrong with the water," said Elenna. "I'd rather go hungry than eat anything that's been in there."

They backed away from the angry river, found some berries to eat with the bread they'd brought, and made camp far from the bank.

"Sleep tight," said Elenna, pulling the blankets over her.

Tom lay down on the hard ground. They had journeyed a long way and he was tired. He stared up at the night sky, where the moon hung big and heavy. But when he closed his eyes he wasn't able to sleep. It was as if he could feel Arax's lurking presence.

He suddenly heard a movement by his feet and sat up with a start. It was Elenna, kneeling with her blanket pulled around her shoulders.

"Are you keeping watch?" Tom asked.

"Well..." Elenna hesitated.

"Get some sleep," he said, grinning at her in the moonlight. "You need to rest as well. If Arax tries to carry me off, I promise to make a lot of noise."

But as Tom lay down again he could hear distant sounds from the mountain. *Is that the screeches of night birds, or something worse?* he thought.

At last he felt himself falling asleep. Tomorrow, there would be a Beast to deal with.

When he opened his eyes again it was a bright morning. There were no clouds in the sky and the sun was warm and golden.

"Breakfast is served," joked Elenna, passing him a handful of nuts and berries.

When they had eaten, Tom got out his map.

"There could be hundreds of caves in this mountain," he muttered. "Which one is Arax's hiding place?"

He quickly scanned the tall peaks. A tiny dark shape appeared on the map and then vanished again into a hole in the side of the mountain.

"That must be his cave!" exclaimed Elenna. "But how do we get to it?" She shaded her eyes and looked at the towering peaks ahead. "I can't see it on the real mountain."

Tom scrutinised the map. "There's a tiny path," he said at last. "It should lead us right to him!"

He scanned the land ahead. When he retrieved the golden armour stolen by Malvel, each piece had given him a special power. The armour was safely back in King Hugo's palace, but Tom had retained its powers. He now used the gift of super-sight from the golden helmet to see a small track snaking up the mountainside. "There it is. Come on!"

He put away the map, jumped to his feet and swung into Storm's saddle. Elenna leapt up behind him.

It wasn't long before they reached the start of the trail, the mountain peaks rearing above them.

Silver stuck close to Storm's hooves as the stallion picked his way over the sharp rocks of the narrow winding path. The route quickly became steep. Soon the foothills were a long way below and there was a sheer drop on one side of the path. On the other side, the rocks rose in a foreboding black wall. A few small plants clung to the cracks.

"We're climbing fast," said Elenna. "It's colder already."

Storm's hooves slithered and slipped on the loose stones. He whinnied in alarm.

"I think we should dismount," said Tom, reining him in. "Storm is the most sure-footed horse I know, but this path is too hard even for him."

"You're right," agreed Elenna, jumping from the saddle after Tom.

Tom took Storm's reins and began to lead him, trying to find the flattest part of the path.

"That's better, isn't it, boy?" he said, patting the stallion's neck. But he noticed that Storm's head was down and Silver's tail drooped between his legs.

"I think they sense the evil around here," Elenna muttered.

Tom gave a shudder. He could feel it as well.

The four friends struggled up the path for what seemed like hours. They kept crossing the same small stream that pounded over the rocks as it snaked down the mountainside.

"This must flow into the Winding River," said Tom. "But look at the water – it's full of angry bubbles, like it's boiling up."

"The weather's changing," said Elenna suddenly. The sky was studded with dark clouds. "And have you seen the birds?" Great flocks were wheeling away from the mountain, shrieking as if in panic.

"They seem to be as scared as the fish," said Tom thoughtfully. As he spoke, the sun disappeared behind a dark cloud and they felt a sharp chill in the air.

"It's spooky here," muttered Elenna. "Do you think we're getting close to Arax's cave?"

"It certainly feels like it," Tom said

with a shudder. He could almost taste the menace in the air. He used his super-sight once more and swept his gaze over the mountainside above them. He could see bare grey rock, dotted here and there with thin, scrubby bushes. And then a deep fissure, like an opening.

"There's something there," Tom exclaimed suddenly. "It's a dark cave, just like the one on the map. That's got to be Arax's hiding place."

They all toiled further up the path. The entrance to the cave loomed black in the shadows like an open, hungry mouth. They were finally in reach of their goal. *At last!* Tom thought. When they stopped, Silver uttered a low growl of warning and Storm scraped his hooves uneasily on the ground.

Tom and Elenna stared at the brooding cave mouth.

"I'm going in," declared Tom. "Aduro and Avantia are depending on me."

He strode boldly to the entrance of the cave. If Arax was watching, Tom wasn't going to let the Beast think he was afraid.

Suddenly Elenna gasped. "Wait, Tom!" She leapt forwards and grabbed his arm, making him stumble back behind her. "I saw something!"

A horrible hissing sound filled the air, and before Tom could react, a coal-black whip shot out of the cave. With a harsh crack it wrapped itself around Elenna's ankles.

"Help!" she cried as she was pulled heavily to the ground. Tom jumped forwards, but he was too late.

Elenna was dragged into the cave and disappeared among the shadows.

CHAPTER FIVE

DEEP IN THE CAVE

A stab of anger shot through Tom. He recognised the whip from the vision Marc had shown them. Elenna was in the clutches of Arax! She was in deadly danger – and all because she'd tried to save him. He had to rescue her.

Tom grasped Storm's bridle, quickly pulled him away to a safe distance, and flung the reins over a spur of rock. Then he called to Silver, who was bristling and growling at the cave mouth.

"Stay with Storm," he ordered. Silver reluctantly settled next to the stallion.

Tom unsheathed his sword and crept towards the cave. Keeping low, he peered inside. It wasn't as dark as he'd expected. Darts of light were showering down from the roof to the floor, giving the cave a strange glow. He could hear the sound of running water.

Tom kept as still as possible, ready for any attack. His heart was pounding as he stared intently into the shadows round the walls. Was Arax lurking there?

He cautiously stepped forwards, treading softly on the rocky ground to make sure his footsteps didn't give him away. Now he could see what was creating the strange, eerie shards of light. A smooth sheet of water cascaded from the roof, tumbling down into a churning pool below. It stretched from one wall of the cave right across to the other.

This water must flow into the Winding River, thought Tom. And if this was where Arax had his hiding place, his evil must be oozing out and flowing down the mountain, poisoning the river below.

"No wonder the fish were desperate to throw themselves free," Tom muttered.

The waterfall gleamed like a mirror – he could even see his reflection in it. There was his face, set and determined. Was he strong enough to defeat the evil Beast that he was about to meet?

I will not fail in my Quest, he vowed silently.

But where could Elenna be? Tom prowled all around the cave, looking behind every rock. There was no hiding place…except behind the waterfall! Tom would have to go through the water to find his friend.

Holding his shield close to his body, he took a deep breath. He was about to plunge through the sheet of ice-cold water when the air was filled with a volley of high-pitched squeaks and clicks. He looked up. A cloud of bats was whirling above him, their leathery wings as black as night. He could see their vicious, pointed teeth as they swooped on him, biting and scratching at his flesh.

He tried to swipe at the creatures with his sword but it was no use. They darted out of the way and then quickly dived at him again. There were too many of them. They swarmed about him like a black cloud and nipped at his skin, making him cry out. Their clawed feet

scratched at his face and their wings slapped against his skin. He caught glimpses of their narrow eyes, gleaming with hatred. How was he ever going to overcome so many attackers?

"The white jewel!" he gasped, as an idea came to him. When he defeated Kaymon the gorgon hound, he had taken a gleaming jewel from the Beast's collar that gave him the power to let his shadow peel away. Now was the time to use it! If he could make his shadow run from the cave, the bats might be fooled and follow it, thinking it was him. Without his shadow he would be unable to move, and in serious danger if Arax appeared, but it was risk he had to take.

Struggling to ignore the scratching

and biting, Tom concentrated hard on the faint outline of his shadow, which lunged and ducked as he avoided another attack from the bats.

Go, shadow! Tom's own words echoed in his head. *Get out of the cave!*

The shadow gave a shudder and wrenched itself away from his feet. It gave Tom a thumbs-up and then rippled along the floor, flitted round the walls and made for the cave mouth. Tom held his

breath. The bats were still swooping and diving, though one of them gave a shriek of anger. Had they noticed the swiftly moving shape?

Tom suddenly felt the seething cloud leave him as the bats tore out of the cave after his escaping shadow. The plan was working!

"I hope Arax doesn't find me here!" he muttered to himself. His forehead was slick with sweat. He wiped a hand across it, and when he looked at his palm he saw in the dim light that it wasn't sweat, but blood. He was bleeding from gashes made by the bats' claws. Scratches covered his head and hands. He had to heal them quickly. The talon given to him by Epos the flame bird would do the trick! He lifted it from his shield and passed it over his wounds.

Each gash disappeared as the Beast's gift touched it.

"Thank you, Epos," he murmured.

Out of the corner of his eye, Tom noticed a sudden movement. He swung round and saw his shadow racing back to him – without a bat in sight! His plan was a success. The shadow leapt through the air with delight. As soon as it was back at his feet, Tom felt himself released from the ground. Now he was free to rescue Elenna.

He took a deep breath and plunged through the waterfall. The cold water made him gasp as it pounded his whole body. Tom took careful steps through the pool. The rocks were slippery and he could only just stand upright under the onslaught.

At last he was through. His face

streamed with water and everything seemed blurred. Then, as his vision cleared, his eyes fell on a figure at the far side of the cave. Dark shadows loomed over her.

"Elenna!" he shouted. "You're alive!"

Elenna stared back at him, her face pale and her eyes pleading silently for help. Now Tom could see cruel claws grasping her round the throat.

That was no shadow looming over his friend.

It was Arax!

CHAPTER SIX

THE GIANT BAT

Tom staggered back. He had seen Arax in the vision at King Hugo's palace, but nothing had prepared him for encountering the Beast face-to-face. Black wings outstretched, the gigantic bat gleamed with pure evil. As his burning eyes met Tom's, he curled his thin lips into a snarl of venomous delight. The crinkled leathery skin was drawn tight over his face, showing the sharp angles of the skull beneath. He tossed his head madly and Tom could see his twisted horns slice through the air. One clawed fist held Elenna in a vice-like grip. In the other was the coal-black whip that he used to ensnare his victims.

Tom could see that Elenna was not hurt, though she was clearly frightened. Arax had been using her as bait to lure Tom into his cave.

The Beast cracked his whip with a cruel slashing sound. It flashed out towards Tom, and he only just managed to dodge the barbs along its length. Tom remembered how Aduro had changed after Arax had taken his soul and the memory made him feel sick. The giant bat's whip could strike him at any moment and he would be stripped of all that was good about him. Aduro and Avantia would be lost.

He had to do something. Tom thought quickly – the golden boots! Their power allowed him to leap higher than any normal boy. He squatted down low, then pushed off

the ground, leaping into the air above Arax's head. He felt the usual rush of excitement that the magic gave him. Taken by surprise, the Beast roared and whirled round, lashing at Tom with his whip. Tom ducked away from each vicious slash.

His plan had worked. With Arax distracted, Elenna pulled herself free and darted away across the cave floor, concealing herself behind a boulder.

Tom landed lightly. Arax flew at him, his huge, black wings stretched to their full span. Tom felt like he was being engulfed by the fearsome Beast. He backed away, but came up against the cave wall. He readied his sword.

I've nowhere to run now, he thought desperately, as he felt the hard rock digging into his spine.

The Beast's evil eyes gleamed with

triumph. He swirled his whip around his sphinx-like head. The black cord went faster and faster, making a high-pitched hiss above the crashing sound of the waterfall. Soon the whip was just a blur in the air.

Tom tried to bring his shield up but he wasn't quick enough. With an almighty *crack,* the whip moved towards him so quickly he didn't have time to react.

A terrible pain flooded Tom's chest. He barely felt his sword and shield fall from his hands as he looked down, seeing a rip in his tunic. The barbs that covered the whip were biting into the flesh just above his heart. Arax gave a victorious shriek and pulled the whip back. Tom gasped and fell to his knees as an icy feeling spread over the wound. The whip had done its evil work.

"I'm coming, Tom," yelled Elenna, darting out from behind the boulder.

"No!" Tom called sharply, his voice faint to his own ears.

He saw her hesitate and step back. She was pulling an arrow out of her quiver, ready to help him if she could.

Tom was trying not to cry out with pain. He turned his shield over and again pulled out Epos's talon. He quickly applied it to the wound. Sure enough, the pain ceased and the wound healed. But before the flesh could close, Tom saw a little wisp of blue smoke escape.

He watched in horror as the smoke rose above his head. He waited to see it soak into Arax's body, just as Aduro's soul had. Instead, the giant bat flicked his whip at the smoke, making it whirl into a tiny tornado.

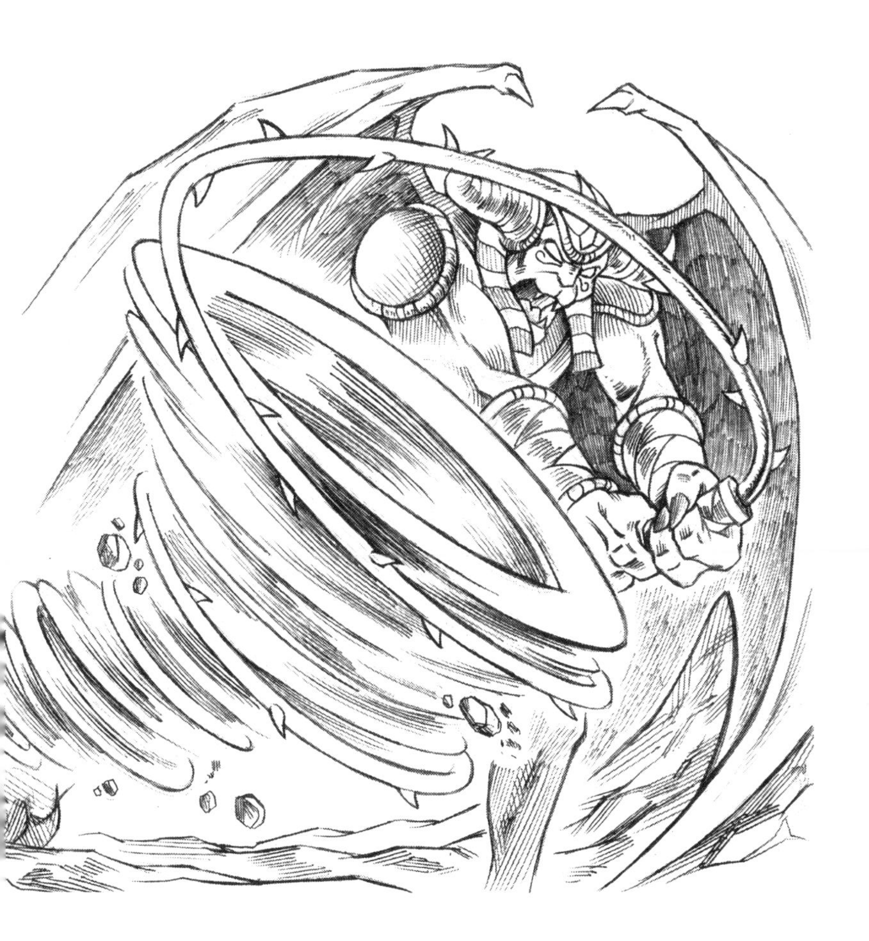

A shadowy figure was taking shape. It grew with each twist of the evil whip, floating towards the wall of water.

"What is that?" cried Elenna.

The smoky blue figure stopped in front of the waterfall. At the same time, Arax gave a screech of triumph, plunging through the water and disappearing from sight.

"We have to get past this thing if we're to find Arax," said Elenna, pointing at the strange figure. "But we don't even know what we're facing."

"Whatever it is," said Tom, getting to his feet, "it won't stop me." He wished he felt as brave as he sounded.

They gazed at the figure, which was becoming more and more solid.

Elenna came close and grasped Tom's hand as its features slowly became visible.

A new enemy had arrived.

CHAPTER SEVEN

A FAMILIAR FACE

Tom felt fear course through him.

Elenna saw him hesitate. "What's the matter?" she asked.

"I couldn't heal the whip's wound in time," he admitted. "I think Arax has sapped some of my strength of heart. I'm not sure I can go on."

For a brief moment Tom saw a worried look pass over Elenna's face.

"Yes, you can," she said firmly. "We're not going to let that Beast win."

Tom still felt uncertain. But then a faint voice inside his mind whispered one word to him: *Taladon*. He thought about the father he had never known. He remembered the tales his uncle had told him about how brave his father had been. While Taladon's blood ran through his veins, Tom would never give in, no matter how frightened he felt.

The figure had passed behind the waterfall and was now reaching out towards Tom through the water. Its finger curled to beckon him.

Taking a deep breath, Tom stepped into the waterfall. The water pounded down on him, flooding his vision. He couldn't see a thing. Calling up all the strength he could muster, he burst through to the other side, with Elenna close behind.

Tom shook the water from his eyes. The figure was standing on a slab of rock. It wasn't a huge Beast but just a boy, the same height as Tom and carrying a sword and shield. He gave Tom a mocking bow.

"It's you!" gasped Elenna.

The boy was almost Tom's double. He was the same height, with the same dark hair, and he stood in a firm stance, just as bold as Tom's.

"He's even got a shield like mine," Tom exclaimed. "Except it's made of leather, not wood."

"Just like Arax's wings," added Elenna. "His eyes are nothing like yours, though. They're evil."

"My name is Nemico," snarled the

boy. "You've met your match at last." His voice was like Tom's, but hard as steel.

A cruel, mocking smile played about his mouth. He reached into his tunic and pulled out a compass. It was identical to the one Tom had. A feeling of helpless rage swept over him. How dare this boy copy his father's most treasured gift! He watched as his enemy flicked the compass open and held it out towards him and Elenna. The needle swivelled round.

Taladon's compass told Tom if he was facing destiny or danger. What would this one say?

The boy peered at the compass, then gave a look that sent shards of ice down Tom's spine.

"Just as I thought," the boy said. He threw back his head and laughed. "The needle points to death!"

RETURN OF A HERO

Dear Friend,

Things have taken a turn for the worse. Despite our greatest efforts, Aduro has felt the bite of Arax's whip and his soul has been stolen. My master has become a danger to himself, and to Avantia. I, who was once his apprentice, have become his guard.

Tom and Elenna are on a Quest to defeat Malvel's Beast, but Aduro grows weaker by the hour. Only if they conquer Arax will Aduro's goodness return to him. Without Tom, we are all doomed. But can he conquer an evil that has already overcome the most powerful wizard in Avantia? Or will our hero lose his essence too?

I hear Aduro calling…I must go…

Marc, apprentice to Aduro

CHAPTER ONE

ON WITH THE QUEST

Tom stared at Nemico. He pulled his shoulders back and so did the boy. Tom's hand tightened on his sword. He watched as Nemico took out his own blade and held it in the same way.

"We're one and the same," Nemico said in a mocking voice. "Only one fights for good, and the other for evil!"

He held his sword in front of him and ran at Tom, slicing the air with his blade. Tom leapt out of the way. The boy was holding up the Quest! He had to find the Beast now.

"Arax!" he yelled. His voice echoed round the rocky walls of the cave. "Come out and face me!" He waited for a moment, but there was no sign of the soul stealer.

"Let's get out of here," cried Elenna. She raced towards the mouth of the cave and Tom leapt to her side, panting to keep pace. If Arax wouldn't show himself, Tom could at least get away from the boy. But it was hard to match Elenna's strides without his strength of heart. It had always kept him going, even when his body was tired.

"Let us pass!" Elenna shouted at Nemico, shoving him aside.

The boy grabbed Elenna and pulled her towards him. He brought an arm roughly around her neck, yanking her back, and placed his sword to her chest.

"If you want to leave this cave, Tom the hero, you'll have to get past me first!" he said. He pressed the blade harder against Elenna, making her gasp. "But who knows what I'll do if you try to escape. Are you willing to risk the life of your friend?"

Tom opened his mouth to speak, but nothing came out. More times

than he could remember, he or his friends had faced danger at the hands of evil. Each time he had looked his enemy in the eye and fought on. But now… Something had definitely happened when the barbs punctured his skin.

He balled his hands into fists. "Leave her alone and fight me!" he shouted.

Cursing the strange heaviness inside him, he ran at Nemico. The boy quickly turned his sword on Tom, jabbing at him with its deadly point. Elenna took her chance and pulled away from the evil boy's grasp. Tom dodged the flashing blade and slammed his shield into Nemico's body. He was relieved to see Elenna slip safely out of the cave.

"Be careful, Tom," he heard her cry.

The boy slashed out angrily at him with his blade and Tom only just managed to avoid the blows.

Desperate to get out of the cave, Tom sliced his sword down through the air towards Nemico, again and again. The other boy leapt backwards to avoid each blow, until at last Tom drove him out onto the narrow mountain path.

Tom's clothes were still wet from the waterfall and the cold mountain air chilled him to the bone. Nemico thrust his sword forwards with deadly intent. Tom moved out of the way just in time, slashing back with all the strength he had. The boy ducked away from the blow easily and came forwards again. He grabbed Tom's sword arm and smashed it against the hard rock.

He's trying to make me drop my sword, thought Tom, as pain shot up his arm. *I mustn't let go.* He shoved Nemico with his elbow, but his enemy rammed him hard against the side of the mountain, forcing the air from Tom's lungs.

He fights just like me, Tom realised. He spun round as quickly as he could, forcing the boy to release his grip.

Tom jumped out of reach, panting to get his breath back. At least the evil boy wasn't getting the better of him – yet. Out of the corner of his eye, he saw Elenna race over to Storm and Silver. She began to lead them further down the mountain, away from the fight, giving Tom a last desperate glance over her shoulder as she went.

At least the animals are safe, Tom thought, as he ducked another vicious swipe from his enemy's blade.

The boy leapt onto a rock and smiled cruelly down at him.

"It must be strange looking at yourself," he mocked. "And to know that I am so much stronger than you. I am not weighed down by your pathetic goodness, you see. Prepare to meet your doom!"

Tom managed to jump out of the

way as Nemico leapt from the rock and aimed a heavy blow at him with the hilt of his sword. How could he defeat this boy? *I've lost my strength of heart,* Tom thought, *but I still have my magic!*

For the first time since he'd been struck by the whip, Tom felt a flame of hope flicker inside him. He would not be defeated! He lunged hard at his foe. Nemico deflected the thrust with his shield.

"Pathetic," the boy smirked. It was as though Tom were looking into his own face – after it had been twisted by cruelty.

Hiss! An arrow flew past the boy's head. And another. Elenna had returned.

Nemico spun round to face her, skilfully blocking each arrow with his leather shield. Tom knew he had to act immediately, but his missing strength of heart had robbed him of the courage to know what to do. Which magic skill should he use?

"Foolish girl!" cursed Nemico.

"You'll be sorry for that!"

The evil boy grasped his shield in both hands and sent it spinning away. It sliced through the air in a deadly arc, whirling straight for Elenna's head.

Tom had to save his friend!

CHAPTER TWO

ELENNA IN DANGER

"No!" yelled Tom as the leather shield flashed towards Elenna.

It slammed against the side of her head with a horrible thud. She toppled and fell to the ground, where she lay completely still. Nemico threw back his head and let out a shriek of triumphant laughter that echoed round the mountains.

Tom stumbled over to Elenna, fearing the worst. She lay seemingly lifeless on the ground. The blow had been ferocious. Had his evil double killed his best friend? The thought struck terror into Tom's heart.

Then, to his huge relief, Elenna gave a low groan and moved her head.

"Elenna," he gasped. "Are you all right?"

She slowly sat up. Tom felt sick. Her face was white and there was a deep wound in her temple that oozed dark blood. She gazed around, as if she were trying to make sense of what had happened, but Tom could see that her eyes weren't focussing properly. Nemico had stopped laughing and now just watched them, a cold smile playing round his lips.

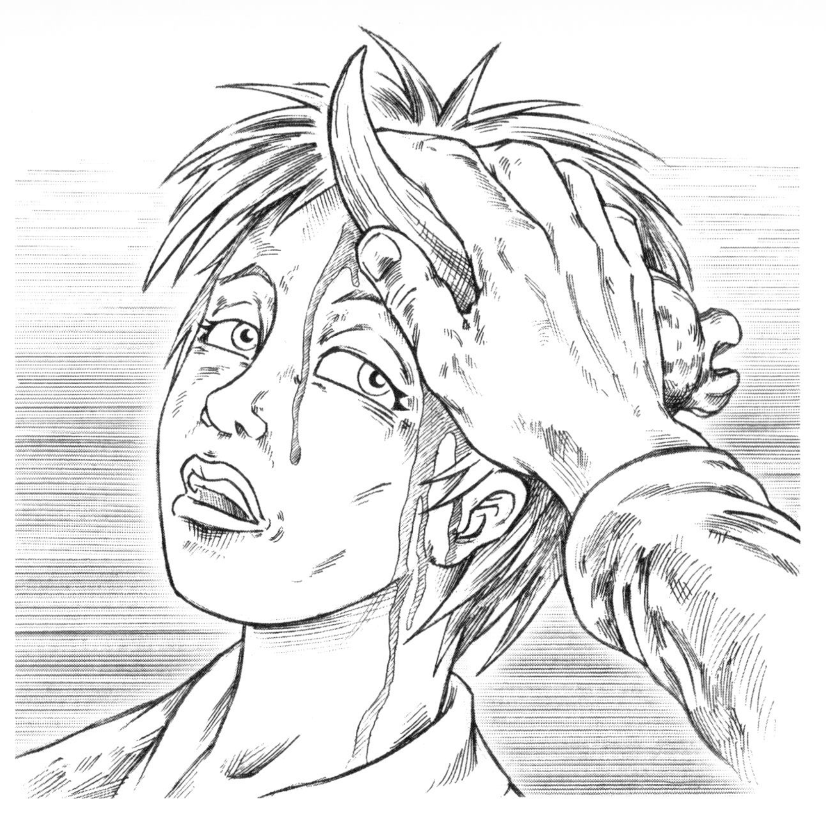

He thinks he's won, thought Tom bitterly. He knew that if Elenna lost much more blood she would soon be too weak to move, and then… He had to act before it was too late. He pulled Epos's talon from his shield and passed it over the gaping wound in his friend's temple. The gash began to glow as it healed before his eyes.

The colour was flooding back into Elenna's face. She looked much stronger now, like her old self.

"Thanks, Tom," she said gratefully. She jumped to her feet and put an arrow to her bow. "He's not beating us," she declared, as she turned to aim at the boy.

Tom felt warm inside. He could sense Elenna's determination strengthening him.

Nemico stood with his hands on his hips looking scornfully at them. "Your arrows won't hurt me," he sneered. "You can't do anything against my skills. I'm too fast for you."

Elenna released an arrow, but Nemico easily threw himself out of its reach. It was clear that he'd stolen some of Tom's quick-thinking and agility.

As Tom watched Nemico roll across the ground, he noticed the boy's leather shield, lying forgotten beside Elenna's foot. Tom darted forwards, with lightning speed, and seized the shield. Without wasting a moment, he hurled it towards Nemico. It went spinning through the air, flying straight and true. As the other boy climbed to his feet, his eyes widened in alarm. Before he could move, the rim of the shield slammed into his stomach, causing him to double up.

Tom had been too quick for the boy, even though the effort of throwing the shield had cost him a lot. Without his strength of heart, every moment of the fight was a struggle. Being a hero was becoming harder by the second.

"Well done!" cried Elenna, encouraging him.

Tom held his sword ready and advanced on the crumpled figure.

"That was a big mistake," Nemico snarled. He scooped up his shield and launched himself at Tom, his sword swishing viciously through the air.

Tom only just raised his own shield in time to parry the blow. He moved round and managed to dodge another sword thrust. But it had been close. *I can't finish this on my own,* Tom thought. *I need help.*

He saw that Elenna had climbed to a flat rock above them. Could she do anything? She was trying to aim an arrow at his double. But Nemico had already proved he was too quick for her. She released an arrow from her bow and it arced through the air, its aim pure and true. But as it dived down towards Nemico, he leapt out of the way, catching the shaft of the arrow and breaking it over a rock.

"Useless!" he called back at Elenna. Her eyes met Tom's and, for a moment, he thought he saw despair.

Tom gazed out over the

mountaintops, stretching away as far as even his magical sight could see. Surely, in the whole of Avantia... And then it came to him – the perfect solution! He would call upon one of Avantia's good Beasts.

A Beast who would be more than a match for this evil boy.

With a grunt of effort, Tom barrelled forwards and rammed his shield against Nemico's shoulder. The boy staggered to one side, crying out angrily. Tom didn't waste a moment. He ran up a slope and gazed out over Avantia, rubbing the dragon's scale in his shield. Then he raised his sword high above his head.

"Ferno the fire dragon!" he called, his voice echoing off the mountains. "I call on you now!"

CHAPTER THREE

HELP FROM THE SKIES

Nemico roared with anger and ran up the slope towards Tom, stabbing viciously at him. The path was so narrow, it was little more than a ledge. One of them could easily fall over the precipice. Tom had to make sure it wasn't him.

The boy's anger had been replaced with a sneering smile.

"You won't last long, Tom the hero," he mocked, striding forwards. Tom had no choice but to back away, and he looked anxiously over his shoulder at the empty air beyond the edge of the cliff. Without his strength of heart, he felt fear coil inside his stomach.

"Why don't you just give in?" asked Nemico, taking another step closer.

Even in his weakened state, the boy's words made Tom hot with fury.

"While there's blood in my veins, you won't defeat me," Tom told his enemy. He scanned the horizon for any sign of Ferno, but the fire dragon's great wings were nowhere in sight.

"You're nothing but a pathetic weakling," jeered Nemico. He brought out his sword and jabbed the point at Tom. Tom leant back and felt himself begin to lose his footing. No! He wouldn't let this happen.

Grabbing hold of a gnarled bush, he managed to right himself, and threw his body at Nemico's, sending the other boy falling to the ground. Their swords clattered out of reach and Tom had no choice but to fight hand-to-hand with his evil double. Nemico was strong and it took all of Tom's last reserves to fight back, pushing the boy off him so he could climb to his feet. He ran to retrieve his sword, and trained the point of it on Nemico.

But where was Ferno? Tom could feel his brief surge of determination ebbing away again, and doubt taking its place. What if the fire dragon didn't come to their rescue? Tom knew he wouldn't have the strength of heart to fight on alone.

A jet of golden fire arced over the mountain peak as the powerful Beast soared into view. He looked glorious, his huge black wings beating the air. He gazed about with a glint in his eyes. Tom felt his spirits soar at the sight of Ferno's gleaming scales and long curling talons.

"Yes!" he heard Elenna cry from her vantage point on the rock.

Tom gazed up at the fire dragon, awestruck. Avantia's good Beasts always made him feel proud and happy. He felt an icy blast of wind

cutting into him, and he was sure he could hear Malvel's cry on the whirling air. It sounded angry and frustrated. Hope began to rise in Tom's heart.

"Arax!" Nemico cried in fear as he sprawled on the ground, staring up at Ferno. "Where are you?" His fingers scrabbled in the dirt for his sword, but Tom kicked it over the cliff edge – far out of reach. He saw the blade glitter as it fell through the air and then smashed against the mountain rocks.

Ferno wheeled round and dived at Nemico, his talons outstretched. He opened his jaws and let forth a fireball as Tom leapt out of the dragon's way, sheathing his sword.

"Help me, Arax!" cried Nemico again. "Arax! Where are you?" He crouched down behind his leather

shield to protect himself as the torrent of fire reached him. The leather melted and peeled away from the frame under the heat of Ferno's mighty breath. The boy angrily threw the shield aside and climbed to his feet. Now he was defenceless.

"You can bring a whole army of dragons," he hissed at Tom. "It won't do you any good. You're *still* going to die!"

As soon as Tom swung his sword at him, Nemico sprang back. But he was on the very edge of the path, and the pebbles beneath his heels clattered down the deadly chasm. The ledge was so narrow, there was hardly any room for him to stand. He swung his arms wildly as he scrabbled away from the edge.

Ferno swooped in for another attack, screeching angrily as he reached out with his talons and opened his jaws. Tom could see another fireball growing at the back of the Beast's throat, ready to be sent out in a fearsome jet. When Nemico saw the dragon hurtling towards him, he threw his arms up to protect himself.

The boy flailed desperately as he teetered on the edge. He glanced at Tom, fear filling his face as the path gave way beneath his feet.

"No!" yelled Tom. He never wanted to see a life lost. Even though this boy was his deadly enemy, he dived forwards and made a grab for the boy's hand.

But he was too late. With a howl of despair, his evil double disappeared over the precipice.

CHAPTER FOUR

THE RETURN OF ARAX

Tom flung himself flat on the path and looked down. The drop was dizzying. But somehow Nemico had not fallen. He was hanging just below the ledge, clinging to a small fissure in the rock by the tips of his fingers. He didn't look as if he could hold on for much longer. His hands were scrabbling and his fingernails were bloody and torn. He looked up pleadingly at Tom.

"Help!" he whispered. "Help me… Please."

Tom leaned over towards him.

"Let him fall, Tom," he heard Elenna call urgently. "He'll only try to kill you again."

Ferno was circling above their heads. He gave a small snort of fire as if he agreed with Elenna.

"Please," came the boy's feeble cry.

His face took on a panicked look as one hand slipped and the fingers of the other began to lose their grip. Tom gazed into the black eyes of his evil double. He saw his own reflection there – it was as if he were looking into his own face.

In that moment, Tom knew he couldn't let Nemico die.

He reached out to grasp the boy's thrashing hand.

"No, Tom!" yelled Elenna.

But Nemico lost his grip. Without another thought, Tom shot his hand out, reaching perilously far over the edge. Nemico stared intently into his eyes as he grabbed desperately at Tom's fingers and held hard.

Tom braced himself to take the boy's weight, but to his surprise he felt nothing. Nemico was beginning to glow. He smiled at Tom, and for once his eyes didn't have their usual wicked glint. His hand slipped through Tom's as if it wasn't there.

"Hold on," yelled Tom.

But Nemico had disappeared, leaving behind only a cloud of blue smoke.

"What's happening?" gasped Tom, pulling back from the edge. The blue smoke whirled about like a coiled spring.

He leapt up and drew back with

a cry. It was the same kind of blue smoke as Arax had used to steal his strength of heart by the waterfall. But Tom couldn't escape it. The smoke was all around him, billowing in great smothering clouds.

Gradually the clouds became a thin spiral that shot into his body through the wound left by the whip. Tom staggered with the force of it. He felt

as if his heart was going to burst and the breath was knocked out of him.

And then he felt – wonderful. His old feelings of determination and strength of heart were returning. He was beginning to think straight again.

"Tom!" said Elenna urgently, running up to him. "Are you all right? What happened?"

"I'm fine," he told her. "I've got back everything Arax stole from me. When I took Nemico's hand, we must have merged somehow. I made the right choice trying to save him. Elenna, don't you see? By saving Nemico, I saved myself as well."

"I'm glad you didn't listen to me, then," said Elenna with a smile.

There was a sharp shriek from the air above them.

They felt the beating of huge dark

wings as the giant bat flew menacingly over their heads. Its bony face seethed with venom.

"It's Arax," gasped Elenna. "He's come for you."

"I have destroyed his evil creation," said Tom grimly. "Now he wants revenge. We'll see about that!"

"Watch out!" yelled Elenna, as the Beast suddenly swooped towards Tom.

Tom stood firm on the path, shield and sword ready.

Whoosh! Ferno came diving down towards Arax. He unleashed a blast of fire that flung the Beast against the mountainside. Then the dragon lunged, claws outstretched.

But Arax was not defeated. He still had his whip. With a hideous shriek, he flicked it straight at Ferno.

The fire dragon bellowed and swiftly changed his course to avoid the whip's evil barbs. It cracked harshly in the air. Ferno wheeled round and sped towards Arax again, lashing him hard with his tail and ripping the flesh of one leathery wing. Arax took to the sky with an agonised hiss, struggling to fly. Ferno rose after him in a flash, screeching angrily.

Ferno had given Tom time to gather himself and prepare for the battle ahead. He knew it was his destiny to defeat Arax the soul stealer – and save Aduro. Tom couldn't bear to think about the good wizard as he had last seen him, writhing in a corner of his rooms back at the palace. He'd do whatever it took to help his friend.

"Thank you, Ferno," he shouted up into the air. He could feel his heart pounding again – there was no need to worry about its strength anymore. "It's up to me now. I must finish this Quest!"

CHAPTER FIVE

IN THE AIR

Ferno flew down and gazed at Tom. His big, honest eyes looked troubled.

"Go," Tom urged him, "and thank you for coming when I called. But now I have to defeat Arax myself." He grasped the hilt of his sword and a surge of power ran through him. The sword felt as it used to – light and strong. With his powers restored,

Tom knew he was ready for anything.

Ferno seemed to understand. He nodded his gigantic head, then opened his wings and took off into the air, making gusts of wind whirl round the rocks. But he didn't fly away. Instead, he circled slowly overhead and came to rest on a high mountain peak.

There he settled, a huge imposing shape with his wings folded about him, watching Tom intently. He may have left Tom to finish the Quest, but it was clear that the fire dragon was not going to abandon his friend.

Tom turned to face his enemy, his sword and shield ready.

"Be careful, Tom," called Elenna, an arrow trained on the giant bat, ready to fire. "Remember, Arax wants you dead."

Tom nodded. "Don't worry," he called. "I've overcome everything he's conjured up. I *will* defeat this Beast."

Arax glared at Tom, his feet stamping on the path. The Beast's evil black eyes seemed to pierce right through him. Then, slowly, the Beast began to advance. In his claws he held his deadly whip, letting it trail behind him like a snake weaving its way over the rocky ground. Then, without warning, he flicked it into life. With a deafening crack, the leather coil sliced through the air at Tom's feet. He leapt out of the way just in time. Again and again the Beast's whip darted at Tom, aiming for his chest and then his head. It was taking all of his skill to avoid another wound from the sharp barbs. Arax laughed wildly as Tom dodged about.

Then Tom saw a new gleam in Arax's eyes. With a single beat of his wings, the Beast flew up until he was hovering above the narrow mountain path. His head lowered, he bore down on Tom with a piercing cry.

Tom saw the long, twisted horns coming closer and closer, and knew the Beast meant to stab him right in the chest. He swung his shield up just as Arax reached him. The Beast's horns were embedded deep in the shield, and he shrieked madly, trying to shake himself free. Tom was dragged about by the frantic movements. His feet slipped at the edge of the sheer drop, sending stones tumbling down the mountainside below. But Tom knew he had the advantage. He raised his sword high in the air.

"For Aduro!" he yelled, bringing his weapon down on one of Arax's horns.

The sharp blade sliced it clean off. Arax gave an ear-piercing screech of pain and shook his head about, wrenching the shield out of Tom's hand. Tom stumbled backwards against hard rock.

Arax lurched around wildly, his claws clutching at the stump where his horn had been. He shook off the shield and it slid away down the path. There was no time for Tom to retrieve it. But he had a plan to get the better of his enemy once and for all. *Where's the best place to be to avoid a strike from Arax's whip?* Tom thought. *On the Beast's back!* He might even have a chance to defeat the Beast from there.

Tom sprang onto a rock and leapt high into the air, towards the black hide of Arax's back.

The giant bat snarled with rage as Tom's legs tightened round his body. His leathery skin felt rough and gnarled. Arax twisted his head, trying in vain to bite Tom's legs, then flailed about uselessly with his whip. Tom knew he would not dare use it. It was too risky. The vicious barbs might get a taste of Arax himself.

I've got him! he thought, and raised his sword to deliver the final blow.

But Arax didn't seem to be beaten yet. Tom felt a great lurch, and the leathery wings surged into flight. He could do nothing but cling on as he and the Beast sped through the mountain air.

"Careful, Tom!" he heard Elenna call out. He glanced down to see her stood on a narrow ledge, firing arrow after arrow into the air. But the missiles were falling far short.

Higher and higher Tom and Arax flew. He could see Storm and Silver far below, tiny as dots on the landscape. Storm was pulling at his reins and Tom could hear Silver's faint frantic howls. Tom saw Ferno stir on his vantage point, watching the battle intently.

The air around him had grown icy cold. It cut through Tom like a blade. He could barely feel his fingers now. How much longer would he be able to keep his grip on the Beast?

He looked down at the fearsome drop. The cave was already far below. The giant bat swooped this way and that, twisting and diving. He seemed determined to shake Tom off and make him plummet to a terrible death on the jagged mountain rocks. Separated from his shield, Tom didn't have the protection from heights of Arcta's feather – and he knew he couldn't survive the fall without it. He definitely had to force the Beast to land. But how?

Arax suddenly turned and swooped upwards into thick grey cloud. The ground beneath them completely disappeared. In the icy mist, Tom lost all sense of where he was. His face and hands felt numb with cold. Arax could be taking him anywhere. There was no time to lose. He had to force the Beast to go back down to the mountain or his Quest would fail.

"While there's blood in my veins," he muttered grimly, "I will not give up!"

Slowly, Tom released his hold from Arax's shoulders and, gripping with his knees, raised himself as best he could on the leathery skin. He still had his sword. If he could just do something to alarm Arax, the Beast might swoop back down to the ground and to safety.

But Arax immediately sensed that Tom was no longer holding on as firmly as before. With a shriek, he shot upwards, twisting this way and that to shake his enemy off. Tom was thrown from Arax's back, his heart lurching as he fell. In desperation, he flung out a hand – and felt it close round the tattered edge of one of the Beast's wings.

His whole body was tossed about as he blindly tried to pull his way back up to the Beast's head. It seemed an impossible task. The wings were smooth and there was nowhere to grip. Then he felt a fold of leathery skin flapping around in the wind. Of course! Ferno's claws had ripped Arax's wings. Using the rips as handholds, he heaved himself back onto Arax's body and was kneeling at last on the Beast's shoulders.

Swiftly, Tom drew his sword, raised it in the air, and struck Arax hard over the head with the hilt. The Beast's body dipped lower as the giant bat lost velocity. He was floating softly to the ground. Tom struck him on the head three more times, forcing Arax lower and lower.

Arax's dreadful shrieks stabbed right through Tom's head. He quickly flattened himself against the bat's back and flung his arms tightly round the coarse, leathery neck, bracing himself for what was to come. When Arax landed, Tom had to be ready for him.

But to Tom's horror, Arax suddenly went completely limp. He began to spiral downwards, dropping out of the clouds on a helpless, tumbling course towards the spiteful peaks of the mountain.

Tom saw the sharp rocks whirling closer and closer as he plunged through the air on Arax's back. Had Nemico been right after all? Was Tom about to meet his death?

CHAPTER SIX

FIGHT TO THE FINISH

Crash! Arax fell heavily onto the mountain ledge. Tom felt the force of the landing jolt through him. His head spun and he could scarcely breathe.

"Tom!" Through his confused thoughts he heard Elenna's terrified cry. "Tom! Are you all right?"

Up in the sky Ferno was circling anxiously.

Tom shook himself. *I'm not hurt,* he realised.

"I'm OK," he called out.

He knew he'd been lucky. Arax had taken the force of the fall. But Tom could feel the Beast's heaving breaths underneath him. *Still alive, then,* he thought grimly. He strengthened his grip on the Beast's leathery back, ready for any move Arax might make.

He could see Elenna running up the path towards them. She looked worried. "Stay back," he shouted. "This isn't over yet."

Arax may have been hurt by the fall, but that did not mean he would give in. And neither would Tom. Aduro was depending on him!

The Beast began to heave himself up, with Tom clinging on tightly. He took a few stumbling steps as if he didn't know where he was. And then Tom realised why. As Arax threw his head back and roared with anger, Tom could see that his eyes were clogged with dust and debris from the impact of the fall. Crashing to the ground had blinded the Beast!

Without warning, Arax flung out a wing and knocked Tom flying.

Tom hit the ground with a heavy thud and rolled helplessly along the path, losing his sword as he went.

"Careful, Tom!" Elenna yelled. "You're getting close to the edge."

Still tumbling, Tom scrabbled about with his hands. Everything was loose and crumbling, but at last he caught hold of a rock. He gripped it tightly and came to a stop, just before he reached the sickening drop.

"Thanks, Elenna," he croaked.

Immediately, Tom realised his mistake. The sound of his voice had given his position away. The ground shook and something heavy fell across his back, forcing the air from his chest, and he was heaved upwards, his stomach lurching. Arax had captured him with his thick leathery batwings. The evil Beast shrieked in triumph.

Tom desperately tried to free himself, but he could barely move his arms and he was finding it difficult to breathe. The wings were clamped hard across his nose and mouth. He was going to suffocate!

Relax, he told himself. *Don't panic. Slow breaths. Take what air you can.*

Then he heard a noise that turned his blood to ice. Arax's whip was slicing through the air. The Beast might be blind and unable to take aim properly, but that wouldn't stop him from lashing out. Tom managed to turn his head so that he could just see the cruel leather strip slicing this way and that. It wouldn't be long before the vicious barbs found Tom.

He heard the crack of the whip again. Tom knew that if ever there was a time to use one of his powers, this was it. Concentrating hard, he called upon the super-strength given to him by the golden breastplate. In one swift thrust, he pushed out with his arms and kicked with his legs.

The sudden movement knocked

Arax off balance, and the whip was flung from his claws, high above them.

But Arax didn't let go of Tom. In his rage, the Beast began to crush him with his wings, squeezing him tighter and tighter. Tom couldn't breathe, and as he looked up he saw another peril coming his way. The whip, its barbs slashing, was loose of Arax's grip and snaking through the air.

It was coming straight for him!

CHAPTER SEVEN

THE DEADLY WHIP

The coal-black whip cracked through the air over Tom's head. Ferno gave a warning call from above.

"Don't worry, Tom!" shouted Elenna. "I'll help you!"

Tom twisted his neck round to look at his friend. He could see that she'd pulled a rope from the bottom of her quiver and was circling it over her head, ready to aim at the whip. But would she be fast enough?

Tom was held in the iron grip of the Beast's wings. He watched helplessly as the whip flashed closer and closer. Elenna released her lasso, and it arced through the air…

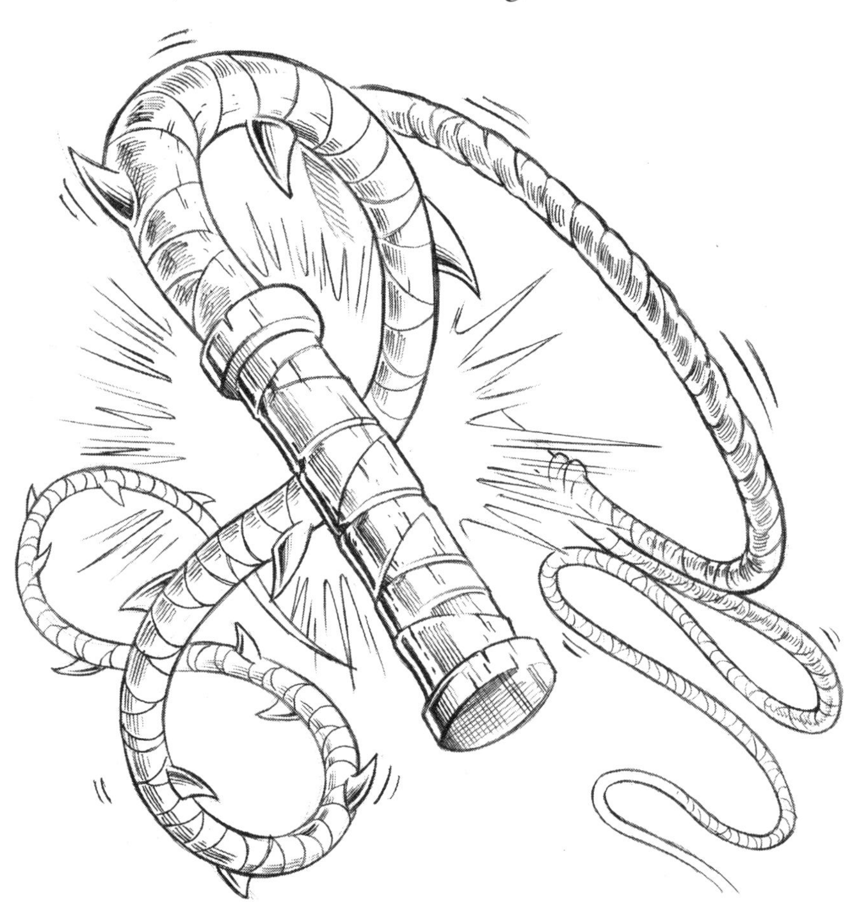

Tom's heart sank as he saw the rope bounce off the whip and fall harmlessly away to the mountain path. To his horror, the whip seemed to be moving of its own accord, snapping and slashing its spiky barbs as it shot forwards. It was headed right for Tom's face.

Desperately, Tom threw his head to one side to avoid it. The leather cord snaked past him and sank its barbs deep into the Beast's heart. With a roar of despair, Arax flung his wings wide – Tom was free! He fell to the ground, rolled to his feet and jumped clear. The Beast raged blindly up and down, the whip dragging after him as he tried to pull it out of his chest.

Arax flung his head back and let out a deathly wail of fear and agony.

Elenna ran to Tom's side. As they watched, a huge cloud of white smoke burst from Arax's chest and rose into the air. The smoke twisted and coiled in a beautiful column, then broke apart into thin ribbon-like strands, glowing with every colour of the rainbow.

"They must be all the souls Arax has stolen," whispered Tom in awe, as the strands spread out and sped away into the distance.

"Do you think they're going back to their owners?" asked Elenna.

Tom nodded. "I think they must be. I'm counting on it if Aduro is to be saved." He ran to retrieve his sword and shield from among the rocks of the mountains. His hand tightened on the hilt of his sword. "And now it's time to finish off this evil Beast once and for all."

He strode forwards, his sword raised ready to attack.

"Wait," cried Elenna, grasping his arm. "Something's happening."

All over his body, Arax's black, leathery skin was curling up like paper in a fire. He was turning to dust! Before Tom and Elenna's astonished eyes, the Beast's flesh and bones were crumpling into a heap. A sudden wind blew up and the dust was whipped around the rocks in a menacing whirlwind. Tom thought he heard a faint cry of fury as the cloud was blown far into the distance over the mountaintops.

"You did it, Tom!" yelled Elenna, punching the air. "You defeated Arax!"

Ferno flew down and brought his huge, magnificent head close to the ledge. His scales seemed to gleam more brightly than ever as his kind eyes gazed into Tom's. At last he gave Tom a gentle nudge with his snout, turned and flew away, his forked tail swishing majestically through the air.

"Thank you," Tom called after the dragon. He knew Ferno was proud of him.

Silver came running along the path and leapt up at him, his tail wagging madly. Tom turned to Elenna with a grin as he ruffled the wolf's grey fur.

"I've never felt so happy to be alive!" he said. "For the first time in any Quest, I began to think that Malvel had sent a Beast I couldn't defeat!"

"But you didn't give up," said Elenna firmly. "Anyway, I don't think that evil wizard can send *anything* which could get the better of you."

"I hope not," said Tom. He looked up to the mountain peaks and shouted at the top of his voice. "I'll still be here, Malvel, no matter what you do!"

No matter what you do… His words seemed to whirl round his head as they echoed off the rocks. Tom heard an angry voice on the wind. He knew it was Malvel.

"Now we must go back to the castle and see Aduro," he said.

They climbed down the path to where Storm was patiently waiting, and unhooked his reins from the rock where Elenna had tethered him. The stallion gave a whinny of welcome. Then he tossed his head and nudged Tom towards the downward path.

"Looks like he's happy for us to get off this mountain," laughed Tom. "I don't blame you, boy."

The air shimmered and a vision appeared. Tom and Elenna recognised the silk robe of the good wizard of Avantia.

"Aduro!" cried Tom and Elenna in delight.

The wizard stood tall and proud, his staff in his hand and his face bright with the kindly smile they knew so well. Although he was still pale, he looked nothing like the evil, snarling creature the two friends had seen back at King Hugo's palace.

"I thank you from the bottom of my heart, Tom," said Aduro. "And you, Elenna – as always you have been his faithful companion on this most deadly of Quests. You have rescued me from a torment that I cannot begin to describe. And I am deeply sorry I caused you such distress when you last saw me. You were brave and true in your fight, Tom, and I am delighted that you are unharmed. Now, someone else would like to thank you as well."

Aduro stepped back to reveal two more people in the vision. They were King Hugo and Aduro's apprentice, Marc. Both were smiling broadly and waved at Tom and Elenna.

"Thank you!" the King called. Marc nodded and waved enthusiastically.

Then Aduro stepped back into view. Tom looked hard at the vision of the wizard. "You seem tired. Will you recover from this?"

Aduro nodded slowly. "In time. And good things have come out of this Quest. I am glad to have experienced the dark forces that are working against Avantia."

"How can you be glad of that?" gasped Elenna.

Aduro smiled. "It has given me new knowledge of the most deadly of

Beasts – Arax. I now understand how he stole the souls of his helpless victims."

Tom frowned. "But Arax has been destroyed...hasn't he?"

Aduro shook his head gravely and the vision began to fade. "I am not so sure. We may yet see the soul stealer return to our realm."

Tom could not stop a shudder running through him.

Aduro raised his staff to Tom and Elenna. "I must rest now. But not before I have thanked a certain fire dragon. Farewell!"

And he was gone.

"Let's go back to the palace," said Tom.

"And have a proper breakfast!" agreed Elenna happily.

They set off walking at a good pace.

Tom tried to ignore the creeping doubt that prickled his skin. Could Arax really return for another fight?

Silver ran up and down the mountain path, barking with delight. Elenna chased happily after her pet. Watching his good friends, Tom felt a surge of warmth and pushed the doubts from his mind. He draped an arm over Storm's neck. How could he ever fail with such companions by his side?

He raised his sword to the sky. "To our next Quest!" he cried.

JOIN TOM ON HIS NEXT BEAST QUEST SOON!

Win an exclusive Beast Quest T-shirt and goody bag!

In every Beast Quest book the Beast Quest logo is hidden in one of the pictures. Find the logo in this book and make a note of which page it appears on. Send the page number in to us. Each month we will draw one winner to receive a Beast Quest T-shirt and goody bag.

Send your entry on a postcard listing the title of this book and the winning page number to:

THE BEAST QUEST COMPETITION:
ARAX THE SOUL STEALER
Orchard Books
338 Euston Road, London NW1 3BH
Australian readers should email:
childrens.books@hachette.com.au

New Zealand readers should write to:
Beast Quest Competition
4 Whetu Place, Mairangi Bay, Auckland, NZ
or email: childrensbooks@hachette.co.nz

Only one entry per child.
Final draw: 28 February 2010

You can also enter this competition via the Beast Quest website: www.beastquest.co.uk

Fight the Beasts,
Fear the Magic

www.beastquest.co.uk

Have you checked out the all-new Beast Quest website? It's the place to go for games, downloads, activities, sneak previews and lots of fun!

You can read all about your favourite Beast Quest monsters, download free screensavers and desktop wallpapers for your computer, and send beastly e-cards to your friends.

Sign up to the newsletter at www.beastquest.co.uk to receive exclusive extra content and the opportunity to enter special members-only competitions. It's the best place to go for up-to-date info on all the Beast Quest books, including the next exciting series, which features six brand new Beasts.

Avantia needs a hero...

It is written in the Ancient Scripts that the peaceful kingdom of Avantia shall one day be plunged into peril.

Now that time has come.

Malvel the Dark Wizard threatens the land with his evil. His ferocious Beasts terrorise the people and will destroy Avantia if they are not defeated.

But the Ancient Scripts also predict an unlikely hero. It is foretold that a boy will take up the Quest to fight the Beasts and free the kingdom of Malvel...

Can YOU survive the BEAST QUEST?

Series 1
BEAST QUEST

An evil wizard has enchanted the Beasts that guard Avantia. Is Tom the hero who can free them?

978 1 84616 483 5

978 1 84616 482 8

978 1 84616 484 2

978 1 84616 486 6

978 1 84616 485 9

978 1 84616 487 3

978 1 84616 951 9

Can Tom save the baby dragons from Malvel's evil plans?

Series 2
THE GOLDEN ARMOUR

Tom must find the pieces of the magical golden armour.
But they are guarded by six terrifying Beasts!

978 1 84616 988 5

978 1 84616 989 2

978 1 84616 990 8

978 1 84616 991 5

978 1 84616 992 2

978 1 84616 993 9

978 1 84616 994 6

Will Tom find Spiros
in time to save his
aunt and uncle?

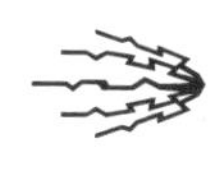

Series 3
THE DARK REALM

To rescue the good Beasts, Tom must brave the terrifying Dark Realm and six terrible new Beasts...

978 1 84616 997 7

978 1 84616 998 4

978 1 40830 000 8

978 1 40830 001 5

978 1 40830 002 2

978 1 40830 003 9

978 1 40830 382 5

Arax has stolen Aduro's soul – and now he wants Tom's...

Series 4

THE AMULET OF AVANTIA

Tom's Quest to collect the pieces of amulet from the deadly Ghost Beasts is the only way to save his father...

978 1 40830 376 4

978 1 40830 377 1

978 1 40830 378 8

978 1 40830 379 5

978 1 40830 381 8

978 1 40830 380 1

All priced at £4.99

Vedra & Krimon: Twin Beasts of Avantia, Spiros the Ghost Phoenix and *Arax the Soul Stealer* are priced at £5.99

The Beast Quest books are available from all good bookshops, or can be ordered direct from the publisher: Orchard Books, PO BOX 29, Douglas IM99 1BQ. Credit card orders please telephone 01624 836000 or fax 01624 837033 or visit our website: www.orchardbooks.co.uk or e-mail: bookshop@enterprise.net for details.

To order please quote title, author and ISBN and your full name and address. Cheques and postal orders should be made payable to 'Bookpost plc.' Postage and packing is FREE within the UK (overseas customers should add £2.00 per book).

Prices and availability are subject to change.